MOMOTARO

(THE PEACH BOY): A JAPANESE FOLKTALE

Retold by M. J. York • Illustrated by Betsy Thompson

The Child's World®
1980 Lookout Drive • Mankato, MN 56003-1705
800-599-READ • www.childsworld.com

Acknowledgments
The Child's World®: Mary Berendes, Publishing Director
The Design Lab: Kathleen Petelinsek, Design
Red Line Editorial: Editorial direction

ISBN 9781614732181
LCCN 2012932427

Printed in the United States of America
Mankato, MN
July 2012
PA02123

Long, long ago in a small village in Japan, there lived an old man and an old woman. The couple was honest and hardworking, and they were mostly happy. There was but one sadness in their lives. They wished every day for a child.

One day, the old woman was washing clothes in the river. As she gathered up her clothes to take them home to dry, a large, plump peach washed up on the riverbank beside her. "A fine peach for supper," she exclaimed. And she picked up the peach and carried it home.

That night, after the couple had finished their rice and tea, the old woman brought the peach to the table. She took up her knife and pressed it against the peach. Suddenly, a voice spoke from inside the peach. "Don't cut me!" it cried.

The old woman and old man jumped in surprise. They had never seen a talking peach before. In front of their eyes, the peach split open. Out sprang a beautiful baby boy.

"Ai!" exclaimed the old woman. She clapped her hands in delight. "It is a child for us to raise! We will call him Momotaro, or Peach Boy."

The years flew by on quick wings. Momotaro grew into a brave, strong young man. On his fifteenth birthday, Momotaro went to the old man and the old woman. He bowed and said, "My beloved parents, I am honored that you have raised me, fed me, and clothed me for fifteen years. Now it is time for me to repay your kindness."

Recently, the village had been attacked by the oni, which were mean and greedy monsters. The oni had stolen food and treasure from the village. Everyone was afraid of the oni, but not Momotaro.

Momotaro explained his plan. "Honored parents, please give me some millet cakes, and I will go out into the world and fight the oni."

The old man and the old woman were worried about Momotaro, but they were also proud of their brave son. The old woman baked millet cakes for Momotaro. The old man found a long, sharp knife for Momotaro to protect himself from the oni.

The family parted with tears. Momotaro went out into the world with his long, sharp knife and a sack full of millet cakes. He followed the long, winding road out of the village toward the island where the oni lived.

It was not long before Momotaro came across a spotted dog. The spotted dog asked, "Momotaro, Momotaro, why have you left your parents? Why are you taking the long, winding road?"

"I am going to fight the oni,"
replied Momotaro.

"And how will you fight the oni?"
asked the spotted dog.

"With my long, sharp knife and the help of my friends," answered Momotaro. "Will you be my friend? I will share my millet cakes."

"I will be your friend and fight the oni," agreed the spotted dog.

And Momotaro opened his sack and shared a millet cake with the spotted dog.

Momotaro and the spotted dog set out together on the long, winding road. It was not long before they came across a furry monkey. The furry monkey asked, "Momotaro, Momotaro, why have you left your parents? Why are you taking the long, winding road?"

"I am going to fight the oni," replied Momotaro.

"And how will you fight the oni?" asked the furry monkey.

"With my long, sharp knife and the help of my friends," answered Momotaro. "Will you be my friend? I will share my millet cakes."

"I will be your friend and fight the oni," agreed the furry monkey.

And Momotaro opened his sack and shared another millet cake with the spotted dog and the furry monkey.

Momotaro, the spotted dog, and the furry monkey set out together on the long, winding road. It was not long before they came across a bright pheasant. The bright pheasant asked, "Momotaro, Momotaro, why have you left your parents? Why are you taking the long, winding road?"

"I am going to fight the oni," replied Momotaro.

"And how will you fight the oni?" asked the bright pheasant.

"With my long, sharp knife and the help of my friends," answered Momotaro. "Will you be my friend? I will share my millet cakes."

"I will be your friend and fight the oni," agreed the bright pheasant.

And Momotaro opened his sack and shared another millet cake with the spotted dog, the furry monkey, and the bright pheasant.

The four friends followed the long, winding road for three days. At the end of three days, they reached a large, still lake. On the shore was a small boat. At the lake's center was an island, and on the island was the oni's castle. The four friends rowed the boat to the island and rushed ashore.

The bright pheasant flew over the tall castle walls and began to peck the oni. The furry monkey climbed the wall and opened the castle gate. Momotaro and the spotted dog ran into the castle. Momotaro slashed the oni with his long, sharp knife, and the spotted dog bit them.

Soon, Momotaro and his friends came to the heart of the castle. There, they met the king of the oni. The king of the oni gnashed his teeth and slashed his claws, but Momotaro defeated him. The rest of the oni fled, never to be seen again in Japan.

19

Momotaro, the spotted dog, the furry monkey, and the bright pheasant found the oni's treasure. There were bright gems and shiny gold coins. There were treasures from Momotaro's village and treasures from faraway lands. The four friends gathered the treasure and took it home to Momotaro's village.

And Momotaro, the old man, the old woman, and the rest of the village lived happily ever after. And the spotted dog, the furry monkey, and the bright pheasant had all the millet cakes they could eat for the rest of their lives.

Japan

FOLKTALES

Momotaro is a popular folktale set in Japan, far away from North America over the Pacific Ocean. The story of *Momotaro* dates back thousands of years, to a time in Japan's history called the Edo Period. In the Japanese language, Momo means "peach," and Taro is a common Japanese boy's name, like Joe or Adam in America. Momotaro together means "peach boy."

A folktale like *Momotaro* is a story that is told so many times that people start to know it by heart. Eventually someone writes it down so other children and families around the world can enjoy it, just as you are now. Folktales are magical, full of adventure, and teach us a lesson about life.

In this folktale, we see magic, or fantasy, when Momotaro first comes to his parents inside a peach. We see adventure in his long journey to the land of the oni monsters. And how does Momotaro get the treasures back from the bad monsters? He has friends—the dog, monkey, and pheasant—to help him. He makes friends with the animals by *sharing* his food, the millet cakes. In this way, sharing is one of the morals, or lessons, of the *Momotaro* story. When we share with others, we make friends. And with friends by our side, we can do great things.

Remember Momotaro's heroic traits, as they may be useful to you one day: courage, in leaving his home for an unknown land; and *perseverance*, or a commitment to his goal, to help him succeed. What other lessons did you learn from Momotaro?

ABOUT THE ILLUSTRATOR

A former educator, Betsy Thompson is now a full-time artist and illustrator. In addition to spending time with her family, Betsy's favorite things include seaside picnics, sunny rainstorms, starry nights, and creating in her studio. Betsy lives with her professor husband and two daughters on the coast of Maine.